# Reaching Out at Henderson's Ranch

a Henderson's Ranch story
by
M. L. Buchman

Buchman Bookworks

# Other works by M.L. Buchman

*Newsletter signup at:*
*www.mlbuchman.com*

# 1

*He reached to console* the frightened villager child.

Stan Corman knew it was dangerous, but he couldn't stop his hand. His left hand kept moving closer though some part of him screamed for it to withdraw, to fall by his side.

The boy, no more than five, could have been his nephew Jack. They had the same tousled dark hair, though Jack's skin was far lighter.

His hand continued to reach.

Deep inside himself, Stan cursed and fought, but his arm moved without his willing it.

No control.

Except his eyes. Though his hand remained out of his control, he could see with his eyes.

Stan could see the little boy's fear—his eyes so wide that the dark irises were almost lost in the vast field of white. He'd knelt so that they were eye to eye. Then Stan looked down and he could see his dog Lucy abruptly sit, close in front of the boy.

Lucy wasn't supposed to sit without a command unless—

Stan's hand brushed the boy's arm.

Lucy whined.

She was a military war dog and was trained to sit and be still when she smelled—

The boy disappeared in a cloud of light that slammed Stan into the void.

The scream tearing out of his throat ripped him from nightmare to darkness.

Absolute darkness…except for the after-image of an exploding boy etched so deeply on his retina that it was all he'd been able to see when he woke in the hospital.

Now, months away, he tried to rub at his eyes as his pulse peaked somewhere past sky-rocket and began a slow fall that Stan knew from experience would banish any hope of sleep for hours.

But there was no hand to rub his eyes with, only a fleshy stump remained of his left hand. His other hand was tangled in the sheets and for a long awful moment he was sure he had lost that one as well. Before he could scream again, he managed to pull it free and pressed his hand to his face.

Five.

He counted four fingers and a thumb pressed from jaw to forehead. Flesh and blood. He could feel them. Five. His right hand still remained intact.

As did the image of the exploding boy.

Stan's life had been saved because the boy's parents—or whatever total bastard had wired the kid up—had rigged the explosives too low. The alignment of explosive and Stan's life had been almost entirely shielded by Lucy's body.

The helmet had protected his head, the goggles his eyes, and except for nasty scarring on his left cheek, the rest of him had been behind armor and dog. Lucy had taken the hit and like a nuclear blast burn image, the shape of her had been imprinted on his lower face and chest in blood and bone fragments. The rest had healed: the dozen broken ribs where parts of Lucy had slammed into him, the concussion from the wall he'd been thrown into so hard that even his helmet hadn't saved him from that. They'd managed to save his left calf and knee with screws and titanium plates, but had warned him it would always be fragile. Just what every SEAL wanted to be labeled: fragile.

He lay in a cot. His pulse had slowed enough—though the rate of his breathing hadn't yet—for him to feel the hard chill of the cabin. The fire had gone out, which meant it was past three a.m.

It was a good sign. Usually the nightmare woke him by midnight in plenty of time to restoke the small cast iron woodstove for the long, sleepless dark watch. He considered waiting until dawn under the covers, but experience also had taught him to get up and build the fire now or the cabin would stay frosty until midday.

A North Carolina boy, his only experience with true cold before now had been on assignment. The Afghan winters had been brutal, but that's where Special Operations said to go—so he and Lucy went.

Lucy.

Shit.

They'd been together for two years in-country. She was six months dead and he still missed her every damn day.

He snapped on a flashlight, for all the good it did him. All he could see right now was the little Afghan boy etched in light. The doctors insisted that it was psychosomatic rather than retinal damage because doctors made shit like that up when they didn't know what was going on. The only part of his vision that he could use for the next hour would be in the one dark, dog-shaped patch that had been Lucy in the lower right corner of his vision.

He swung out of his bunk, tipped his head back and to the side so that he could see where he was going, and crossed to the woodstove. Grabbing the handle without a hot pad had him yelping again—not pain but a sharp, panicked sound that rang harshly in the small cabin. If he damaged his right hand he'd be beyond fucked. It was all he had left. He sucked on the slight warmth on his palm as if it was a second-degree burn, cursing the damn stove for still being hot to the touch, but not heating the cabin.

Reaching with his other hand didn't help. The paired titanium hooks of his prosthetic arm didn't care about the heat, but he hadn't pulled the rig on and all he had to wave about was his fucking stump.

Fumbling toward the woodpile, which was on the side he couldn't see, he found a small log and used it to whack the metal handle upward and swing the door open. For its duty and fine service, he chucked the log onto the few remaining embers inside.

Raising one knee, he propped a small bellows on his thigh and pinned its lower handle in place with his stump. With his remaining hand, he worked the upper handle until he coaxed a small snap of flame to life. It was bright enough to shine through the boy's afterimage. Carefully stoking the fire, he watched the flame grow as the boy faded.

The stove wasn't throwing much heat yet; all of the iron had cooled…except the goddamn handle. But he didn't move away. His bare skin rippled with goosebumps, but he remained to watch the flame.

When he'd first come to this small cabin in the Montana foothills, he'd spent many nights contemplating throwing his fake arm into the fire and then himself. At first he only resisted because he knew he'd piss off the ranch owner, and you didn't piss off a man like Mac Henderson or his son Mark.

Mac was a former SEAL—except he'd done his twenty years and retired. Being a SEAL, it was an easy bet that Mac would have followed Stan straight into hell and dragged him back to whup him good for throwing away the gift of life.

*Gift of life, my ass.*

It was early April. Back in North Carolina, the Sweet William would be blooming right now. The cherry blossoms would have already had their spring and the young cottonwood leaves would be unfolding to seek the sun.

Instead, he was squatting in front of a cold fire in a ramshackle cabin on the edge of the Montana wilderness surrounded by snow. It wasn't the life he'd pictured. But the life he'd pictured had thrown him out on his ass. When he'd gone home, his mother had burst into tears every time she looked at him. His fiancé hadn't even bothered to Dear Stan him. True love hadn't even lasted out the month for the half-man he'd become to make it out of the hospital. His sister had forced Stan's brother-in-law to offer him a pity-job at the bank, as if Stan would be forever helpless. Besides, there was no way he could ever survive working indoors. And young nephew Jack had taken one look at his steel hooks and run away screaming in terror—as terrified as the little boy in the Afghan village.

Then one day he'd gotten a call from his former CO to come over to Fort Bragg. It was the last place in the world for a one-armed former SEAL to be, but saying no to Lieutenant Commander Luke Altman wasn't something a man did.

Altman had met him at the gate, which was a real favor. It saved him having to kill every damn grunt who stared at the hooks sticking out of his shirt sleeve and gave him that you-ain't-a-soldier-no-more look.

"Got someone I want you to meet."

"I don't need another goddamn therapist or perky wounded warrior volunteer to tell me how to live with myself."

Altman had merely looked over at him in that long, quiet way he had and Stan shut up. Altman took him to the SWCS dining hall. It was strange to be back on the JFK Special Warfare Center and School grounds and not be ragged from their typically brutal training scenarios. He hadn't let himself go after getting released, but he hadn't done a decent work-out either—not with one fucking hand. The month on his back had cost him a lot of muscle and the PT hadn't really put it back on—weird to trade the military's Physical Training acronym (or Puking Torture depending on who was leading the drill) in for medical's Physical Therapy, which told him just how civilian he'd become.

They grabbed trays and went down the line. Stan had learned enough about working his hooks to not need any help. Actually, having been left-handed before the injury, he was almost better with the hooks than with his clumsy right hand. It had become almost natural that when he extended his arm, or flexed his opposite shoulder, the two hooks separated and when he withdrew or relaxed they clamped together tight. Stan used them to load up on he didn't care what and went to sit with another pair of civilians—the ex-military kind by the look of them.

"Stan Corman. This is Mark Henderson and Emily Beale. Former Night Stalkers who founded the 5D."

Okay, that got Stan's attention.

The Night Stalkers Special Operations Aviation Regiment specialized in helicopter transport for soldiers like him—like he'd been. He'd flown with SOAR plenty of times, but never with the 5D. They were practically legendary and were always with the very top teams, Delta and DEVGRU. He hadn't known one was a woman, but nothing surprised him about the 5D. If these were the founders… But shit! They were still intact. What was their goddamn excuse?

"They," Altman was still yammering, "have a place that they're going to tell you about. His dad runs the ranch and Mac trained me back in the day. Stan, you're going to shut up and listen."

Shutting up and listening had never been his top skill, but not arguing with his CO—former or otherwise—had been too ingrained, especially when it was SEAL Commander Luke Altman.

And that meeting had led to him squatting naked in front of a woodstove at the far corner of Henderson's Ranch in snowy April.

The dawn had happened at some point while he watched and fed the fire. The purging by flame no longer beckoned to him, but its warmth didn't comfort him either.

He was never going to fit back in. His dog was gone. Two of his team also had been close enough that they'd gone home in a box. The other two had gone down in a hail of crossfire that filled two more boxes. Left for dead; he'd been the "lucky one."

The lucky one.

No team. No unit. No longer a soldier. He'd lost fiancé, family, and town.

There was no one who wanted him. No place he belonged. The dead end was staring him in the face and there was no reverse gear out of it. His future was bricked in as surely as the sides of the glowing iron box filled with ashes and fire. Who would give a shit if the flames did consume him? Easy answer. The future held noth—

A knock sounded on the cabin door. The sudden sound where there shouldn't be any sent him diving for cover behind the woodpile. All it earned him was a couple of splinters before he recovered and remembered where he was.

Furious with himself for sliding back into the black hole of panic and depression, he strode to the door and reached for it with his stump, then yanked it open with his right hand and a snarl.

Ama Henderson stood there with her horse tethered to the porch rail behind her. Mac's wife was a tall, magnificent woman. Her skin was still dark and smooth, but her hair had turned that dark steel-gray that was so unique to her Cherokee heritage.

"May I come in?"

It was a several-hour ride from the main house to the cabin that they'd given him; a damned cold one. The sun…he'd lost time again. It was a couple of hours above the snowy horizon in the crystal blue that was a Montana winter sky.

He held the door wider and the chill wind wrapped around him and reminded him that he was naked.

"Shit! Excuse me." He left Ama to close the door as he dragged on some clothes as well as he could. They were icy cold because he'd dropped them on the floor last night rather than on the chair by the stove. Without his arm on, it proved impossible to pull on underwear and pants.

Hating it, he stood there naked and dragged on a t-shirt first. He couldn't stand people seeing him put on his arm—not even the docs who'd fit it and trained him—but he had no choice. He found the thin cotton sock and pulled it up over his stump, careful to smooth out any wrinkles despite his haste. Then he unsnarled the harness, slipped his stump through one loop and into the socket of the prosthesis. With a practiced lean, he managed to get his good arm through the harness' other loop on his first try, thank god, and shrug it on. Now able to control the spring action of the paired hooks, he was able to drag on underwear, socks, and pants. A heavy jacket against the still cool cabin—he hadn't closed the woodstove's door and damped the fire to get good heat from it—and then he jammed his feet into his boots, though he'd be damned if he'd demonstrate for anyone how clumsy he still was at lacing them.

When he turned back, Ama was sitting at the small table looking down into a bundle she'd been carrying. Kind enough to offer him privacy while he struggled.

"Sorry, Ama. Can I offer you some coffee?"

He kicked the woodstove door shut, almost losing one of his unlaced boots into the fire in the process.

"No. I have come to offer *you* something."

As he'd learned was typical with her, she didn't say much but when she did, there was no point in either interrupting or attempting to hurry her to the point. So, he sat in the other chair and waited.

She looked at him with her intensely dark eyes. "You have decided that you don't want to stay at the main compound. I can respect that. There are times that a man must face his future alone. But there is also a time for that to end. My husband would leave you until spring to stew in your own thoughts. By then the pot will boil over. I do not choose to leave you so long."

He readied his protests that he wasn't fit

to be neighbor to man or beast. His screams alone as he rose from each night's dreams were proof enough of that. What if they never ended? What would he do then?

Apparently done with what she had to say, she stood and headed for the door leaving her bundle on the table.

"Ama. I—" he called after her, but the bundle on the table moved.

In the moment of his distraction, she was gone out the door. He knew that even if he rushed after her, she would somehow be gone, departing as quietly across the snow as she'd arrived.

The bundle moved again.

Then a nose stuck out the top.

It sniffed the air once, twice, then the rest of the head emerged and the puppy turned to look at him. Its dark face wore the goofy grin that could only be a Malinois—the same breed as almost every war dog. The same breed as Lucy.

Stan stared at it in horror, not even able to tear his eyes away to look at the door where Ama Henderson had left him.

A dog.

He couldn't even care for himself; how was he supposed to care for a dog?

The puppy yipped at him and he flinched.

It wasn't fair. He would end up killing it just as his one mistake had killed every other good thing around him.

# 2

*Freshly weaned and only* partially house-broken, the dog soon had Stan far more occupied than he'd been on any day in his three months at the cabin.

His usual day's activity was to work on fixing up the cabin—that's how he was paying his rent. It was a fishing cabin in the summer for tourists and it showed. Years of wear and tear had battered the place hard. He'd started with the kitchen. Figuring out how to hold a measuring tape had been a challenge at first but was trivial compared to saws and hammers. With practice, he was getting the hang of it and had made slow but steady progress. Something that had been one motion might now be three, but there was no rush. And once he figured out how to do each task, he moved along well enough. Except the screwdriver was going to send him to the nuthouse; he just didn't have the manual dexterity retrained into his right hand yet.

But the first thing the puppy did once he'd lowered it to the floor—Stan used the blanket the pup had come in so that he didn't have to touch it—was to race around the room about twenty times and then pee on Stan's only clean pair of socks. A second later, the furry whirlwind had chomped down on the leg of a pair of Stan's jeans and begun wrestling them into submission.

He'd forgotten what an insane chewing machine a young Malinois was. He spent the next half hour racing to keep a step ahead of the puppy. He'd pick up one thing and the puppy would discover another. His hand was as big as it was or he'd have swatted the damn thing aside to just give him a single goddamn moment of peace. When his leather tool belt had become the next great find, Stan gave up and let him have at it.

Him. At least Ama had given him that bit of kindness. If it had been a female Malinois, he didn't know if he could have looked at it without breaking down. But like Lucy, it had classic markings. A little smaller than a German Shepherd, instead of a black Shepherd back, it had a black face. And instead of growing into its paws, a Malinois grew into its upright ears and this dog was going to be big—which meant the puppy looked like he was half rabbit.

When the puppy had finally convinced the leather tool belt just who was the king of the cabin, he ambled over and plunked his bottom down beside Stan's boot and began tipping its head one way and another as it inspected the laces.

"Oh no you don't," he stomped his foot, sick of the damn thing.

The pup looked up at him and back down at the boot without startling away.

That gave him pause. "What do you think of this?" He rapped his hooks sharply on the table top.

The pup looked up at the underside of the table for the source of the noise and then its eyes tracked back and forth between him and the table.

Stan rapped again.

This time the puppy watched him instead of the location of the noise.

"Smart little fella, aren't you?"

In response to his compliment it jumped up and yipped in delight. Then it raised a leg to pee on his boot.

In a single motion, Stan scooped it up with his good hand, two steps to the door, and he tossed it into a snow drift.

That turned into another excuse for a dozen circles and then it peed where the front porch post disappeared into the now yellowing snow. It eyed the low steps with some confusion, but had soon struggled back up onto the porch. Once it reached him, it sat and tipped its head as it stared up at Stan to see what he would do next.

Stan looked down at his good hand and flexed his fingers against the strangeness. It was the first living thing he'd touched since the Afghan boy. He tried to wipe off the sensation on his jeans, but the warmth wouldn't go away.

Stan spent some time gazing out at the hoof prints in the snow that proved Ama Henderson had indeed been here and he hadn't imagined her. He looked down. He hadn't imagined the goddamn dog either.

# 3

**Stan reached out.**

The little boy looked so scared.

Five Special Ops soldiers were enough to scare anybody. It was kind of the point. Lucy, fifty pounds of war dog, was no less daunting a sight. Her body armor included goggles against wind and sand, and a Kevlar vest that also sported a camera that could feed visible and infrared imaging directly to a screen that Stan wore inside his wrist. She also had pouches for food, water, and doggie first aid. To the little boy, used to painfully lean feral mutts, she probably looked as alien as the soldiers did. She could work on or off leash, but in the village he kept her on the long lead, more for the villagers' peace of mind than for any real need.

The boy sidled closer as the team eased forward across the village square. It was the edge of evening, the worst visibility for the locals. There was a rumored Al-Qaeda nest two blocks up and one block over. Their team was being sent in to roll it up and look for any intel.

He and Lucy worked to make sure there weren't any IEDs in their path. Check that— they *knew* there were IEDs; it was up to him and Lucy to tell the team where.

The boy came closer, desperately clutching a toy truck. He was close enough for Stan to see that it was a real toy, not just some piece of scrap metal turned into a pretend truck. He knew that was a clue of something, but he couldn't come up with what.

To get down to the boy's height as he edged closer, Stan took a knee—placing one in the dirt, his other raised with his foot planted so that he could push off into a sprint if called.

He reached toward the boy, saying meaningless noises to calm him.

*Take them back!*

But he kept murmuring.

*Shoot him! Chase him away! Scare him!* The boy was on the edge of running away in fear as it was.

Instead he beckoned, calling the boy closer, easing his fear rather than adding to it.

*No! Run! Hide!*

Lucy stepped up close, sniffed the boy, and planted her butt down between them.

*He'll kill me!*

Lucy whined.

*The truck is a bribe! A real toy as a gift to make the kid overcome fear!*

And in that instant, something landed on his chest like a hard punch.

Stan swung at it and missed.

Stump. No hand.

He pulled his other hand free of the blanket and grabbed hard onto whatever had hit him.

A sharp yip of surprise and pain. For a brief instant he held a handful of struggling fur.

Fur far softer than Lucy's.

A puppy's fur.

He let go and could hear it scrambling away across the cabin.

Shit! Stan struggled up from the bedding. The cabin was still warm. He hit the flashlight and checked his watch.

It was one the same wrist as the hand holding the flashlight.

Twenty-two hundred. The dream had given him less than an hour of sleep this time.

But he could see the cabin without tipping his head like the goddamn dog. No explosion apparently meant no afterimage. That was a first.

He went searching for the puppy and finally found him cowering under one of the bunks Stan hadn't fixed up yet. He had to lie down on the rough wooden floor, which was not all that warm, to reach in and snag the pup.

He nipped Stan's hand, but didn't even break skin. Stan had enough scars from training Lucy and other dogs that puppy teeth didn't phase him.

Sitting back down on the bed, he calmed the pup. Telling it he was sorry. Gods, he was sorry for so much. The puppy forgave him quickly enough, planting both front paws on Stan's chest to reach up and lick the bottom of his chin.

If only Stan could forgive himself.

# 4

*Early April had melted* into mid-May before there was another knock on the door.

It didn't send him diving for the woodpile this time. It also explained why the pup had gone up on point, but remained dead silent—just as trained. He took to instruction quickly. Usually the first couple years were about little more than socialization and basic behavior. The pup had taken to commands as if born to them.

He bent down to pat it on the head which was now up to his knee rather than at mid-calf where he'd started.

"Good boy." He really had to name the dog, but that would make him too real, too important. Besides, with only the two of them in the cabin, it wasn't as if there was any confusion about who was talking to who.

Stan pulled open the door and Mac Henderson was standing on the other side of the threshold. He was a big man, still powerfully built though he was in his late sixties. His hair, unlike his wife's dark steel, was almost pure white. It gave him a grandfatherly look, but his handshake was still a force to be reckoned with.

"So," he looked down, "that's where Bertram got to."

"Bertram?" Stan asked the dog and the quick thumping of its tail said that the name had found the dog already.

"Ama brought him by."

Mac winked. "Ama's a sneaky one, isn't she?"

"No, she's…" Then he started thinking about the person he'd been six weeks ago compared to the one now. No diving behind the woodpile. Half of the time the pup— Bertram—woke him before the nightmare could take him back under. A couple nights he'd actually just slept through. On the nights it did strike, he rarely woke screaming, though the shakes and adrenaline were still there. He'd snap his fingers and the pup would hop up and join him in the narrow cot and sometimes he could even get back to sleep. Maybe Ama was sneaky.

"Told ya," Mac nodded with satisfaction. "Let's see what you've got done." They spent about half an hour touring about the small cabin. Stan had done more than merely resetting drawers and renailing ladder rungs up to stacked bunk beds. He'd sanded and refinished all of the trim. The kitchen shone. The fine oak that he'd discovered on the bed rails now had a warm glow to them. The gray patina of old wood that had built up over the years had been banished. There was still more to do, plenty more, but he was pleased and so was Mac.

The friendly thump on his back, despite the reminder of the crisscross of his prosthetic's harness, was appreciated.

"I can see that I need to maroon more SEALs in remote cabins around about here."

Stan decided that it had certainly worked for him, when he was sure that nothing else would.

# 5

***It was the end*** of May when the storm hit.

Stan and Bertram had gone for a final hike up into the hills. Two more days and he'd have to move out. The cabin shone, ready for the paying customers to feel they were roughing it out here.

Funny, Stan had just assumed they'd keep him on, give him a place to fit in. In his mind, he'd been sure of it. The itch between his shoulders? Not so much. Could he make it back in nowhere, North Carolina? No. That home was gone. He'd have to find somewhere fresh. Start over. Start over with Bertram?

The dog belonged to the Hendersons and was showing real potential.

Shit! Once again he was a half-man with no future. Would he ever find a road to a whole new life? One where he wasn't himself? Apparently not. He had to laugh.

"Too damn scared to try," he told the dog. "Wouldn't that just piss off Altman?" Oddly, Stan realized he would piss himself off too. Maybe, just maybe, he could do this. Find some place…God knew where.

He chucked a stick for Bertram, who raced off through the tall meadow grasses to kill it and drag it back. At first he'd been as clumsy throwing with his right arm as a teenage girl *trying* to look helpless. But he'd slowly gotten the knack of it—the dog had been willing to help him get plenty of practice.

About an hour later, far up beyond the cabin, and the fishing stream that ran close behind it, a long set of falls climbed to an upper lake. They weren't one single drop, but a series of cascading white water separated by brief pools. Bertram loved to plunge into those, despite the glacial-fed chill, and they came up here often.

Today they'd reached the lake for a last look around. A pair of elk, mother and calf, were feeding along the lake shore. He called Bertram to heel. The pup obeyed, though he quivered with excitement as they watched the two goofy looking animals drink and then amble into the freezing lake as if it was a warm bubble bath.

A chill across Stan's shoulders had him turning from watching their play.

The sky to the west had turned dark, almost black. He blinked at it in momentary confusion. To the east, the Montana skies were still a brilliant blue. The cabin was a cheery spot far below. He'd even gotten a fresh coat of paint on it, sky blue with dark green trim, so it really stood out in the meadow of spring grasses and wildflowers.

Back to the west, the darkness was boiling closer and the temperature was plummeting. He hadn't even brought a jacket, just thrown on a t-shirt and gone walking.

Time to get his ass moving. They were at least an hour from the cabin and the storm would be on them in minutes.

Another glance filled him with disbelief.

This wasn't some rainstorm, the ground below the leading edge was turning white. Snow at the end of May? It didn't make any goddamn sense, certainly not in North Carolina or Afghanistan. Sensible or not—it was coming.

He was halfway down the steep path along the falls when it hit. The blizzard slammed into him with hard winds. In moments, it was a whiteout.

Keep moving.

"Only dead men stop moving," one of Altman's favorite phrases.

Bertram was doing far better than he was. Atop his thick fur Stan had fashioned a vest in roughly the pattern of a war dog's armor. It carried water, dog snack, and first aid—a good training tool that was now buffering him from the elements.

The path was soon obliterated and he had to slow his pace. His instinct to chafe his arms proved stupid. Rubbing his left with his right, all he felt was plastic and wire. When he tried the other way, all he got were freezing metal hooks scraping up and down his good arm.

Useless.

Broken half-man.

At the third waterfall, he must have veered off the path. He didn't even have time to cry out before he was plunged into freezing water. The only thing that kept him from going over the biggest drop of them all, were his hooks.

His right hand was already numb from scrabbling through the snow. But the metal hooks didn't care about temperature and instinct had him jamming them into a crack in the rock. There was no screaming strain on his arm muscles either. The harness took the load and distributed it to the straps across his shoulders. They were narrow and bit in, but they held.

Forty feet of tumbling waterfall crashed loudly on the rocks below. Even if he couldn't see the bottom through the snow, he could hear the water pounding on the jagged rock fall. As he clung there, it struck him just how easy it would be to give up—just…let go. Then it wouldn't matter that he had no place he belonged, he'd be gone.

Then Bertram whined at him.

And for the first time outside his dreams, Stan knew fear. Real fear.

He'd felt anger at everything he'd lost. He'd

felt betrayed by his family and by the military. But to die now? To leave Bertram? To not look at the cabin again—a job well done—or heave a branch for the dog to bring back? That would be a tragedy.

He dug in, hauling himself up through the freezing water, mostly with his hooks. He found a purchase for a boot, and felt blessed that he'd finally gotten good at tying laces.

When he eventually rolled up onto the trail, he knew he was screwed. Still half an hour to the cabin even under normal conditions, soaking wet and shivering in the snow. He was going to die of hypothermia right here.

He started to laugh. It was a crazed, hysteric sound, but he couldn't stop it. He'd survived SEAL training. He'd survived being blown to pieces in a remote Afghan village. And he'd survived his own self-destructive thoughts.

A late snow on a Montana ranch was going to be what killed him. Fucking snow.

Bertram licked at his face as if he wasn't already wet enough.

"Why can't your name be Lassie? Then I could say 'Get help' and you'd race the miles back to the ranch in time to save me."

Stan tried going fetal to conserve what little warmth he could, but the plastic arm didn't help.

Then something tugged at his belt.

Bertram. He'd never gotten over gnawing that first belt into submission.

The dog yanked at him again.

"Go away. Now isn't the time to play."

Bertram answered with a hard growl and tugged at the belt hard enough that Stan actually slid a foot down the trail.

"Goddamn it! Cut that out." Stan waved an arm at him.

When the steel connected with dog, he yipped in surprise, then answered with a hard snarl and clamped down on his forearm with a fighting hold.

If it had been his real arm, he'd have torn muscles and streaming blood from the force of the attack.

"Release!" He shouted through the roar of the storm's wind.

Great.

Snow wasn't enough, he needed a wind chill to make sure he was a goner.

Bertram let go, but didn't back off.

When he didn't move, the dog took a step in again.

"No you don't!" Stan forced himself to move.

"Only dead men stop moving." Goddamn Altman.

But he *was* moving which meant he wasn't dead. For the first time in far too long he really didn't want to be dead.

He flailed out with his hooks, and this time managed to catch the lift-loop he'd stitched into the back of Bertram's vest. It was used when a dog had to be lifted and carried, or winched up into a helicopter. He'd made the loop strong, the one surviving portion of the leather tool belt that a new puppy had defeated on his first day.

"Go," he croaked out the command. "Cabin."

Bertram turned and dug in. He wasn't big enough to make much difference, but he was still a force in the right direction as long as Stan didn't unclamp his hooks from the lift-loop.

At first, he could do little more than crawl as Bertram dug in with all fours. But he finally found one foot and then the other.

He wished he could say he didn't remember the rest of the trip back to the cabin, but he did, every grueling second of it.

His morning cooking fire had kept the cabin warm. And even that remaining bit of warmth was enough to sustain him through restoking the fire, stripping, and crawling into bed.

Unable to snap his fingers, he stuttered out the dog's name and Bertram climbed in beside him. He too was shivering.

Stan held him close, hard against his chest, but the dog didn't complain.

He buried his face in the dog's fur and knew he could never let go. He and Bertram were a team. They would find a way through, together.

Bertram licked at the salt running down Stan's cheeks before they both fell asleep.

# 6

*"I had this crazy* idea."

Stan sat on the verandah of the big house, a beer bottle pinched securely between his hooks, and his good hand rubbing Bertram's ears.

Mac sat on the dog's other side and they both faced out across the ranch. It was now busy with the first of the June tourists trying to prove they could ride a horse around the corral and being shocked as shit that they actually could.

"Let's hear it," Stan was open to any ideas at this point.

"Back in my day, we didn't have the dogs. Left them behind in Vietnam and didn't need them again until Iraq and Afghanistan."

Stan knew about that. The entire program had been lost for thirty years and had to be rebuilt from scratch. Same thing had happened between the World Wars and again until Vietnam. The military swore that wasn't going to happen again, but he knew the main training center down at Lackland Air Force Base was already feeling the budgetary pinch with the supposed end of Iraq and Afghanistan.

"Now the Special Ops dogs, they're special, aren't they?" Mac asked it as half a question. Clearly he already knew the answer.

"Sure. They're trained by select contractors rather than going through the standard Lackland program. We—" Stan practically choked, had to sip his beer to clear his throat. "They, the Spec Ops, need dogs with more skills than the standard program gives them, no matter how good it is."

Mac nodded sagely. He gave Bertram a rough rub on the head and the dog sighed happily.

"Takes a lot to run a ranch. A lot to keep it afloat."

"Hell of a spread you've built here," Stan agreed going along with the subject change. He'd spent the winter and spring out at the fishing cabin. It was only now that he was seeing the horse wranglers, the recreation directors, the kitchen staff, and all the others it took to run the place.

"Still haven't figured out what I'm going to do with that patch of pasture," Mac waved off to the south of garage. "There's also a lot of room to try crazy ideas."

"Such as?" Stan still didn't see where the old man was heading.

"You trained Bertram up a treat," which sounded like another subject change.

"Thanks," Stan wondered when the man would find his point, but he was just as wily as his wife on working his way there, so Stan waited a little longer.

Mac stood up and stretched. Finished his own beer and tossed it in the small bin on the porch with a sharp rattle of glass.

Stan watched him walk down the front steps and head for the horse barn.

He could barely hear Mac's final words as he walked off toward the barn, "Bertram has five brothers and sisters. Come along if you want to look 'em over." Then he kept walking.

Five brothers and sisters? A whole litter of Malinois? And enough room to train them. He looked at the south pasture again. There was plenty of space for him to build an obstacle course for the dogs. Maybe even a training center for the handlers. Stan could see it clear as day.

He looked at the old man and then down at the dog who had tipped his head to watch Stan and see what he'd do next.

"Bet they barely know how to fetch. What do you think? Want to train up your litter mates?"

Bertram leaning in for another head scratch was all the answer he needed.

He tossed his empty, rolled to his feet, and slapped his good hand against his thigh. Bertram leapt down the steps and they headed out to the barn together to see what the future looked like.

# About the Author

***M. L. Buchman has*** over 40 novels in print. His military romantic suspense books have been named Barnes & Noble and NPR "Top 5 of the year" and *Booklist* "Top 10 of the Year." He has been nominated for the Reviewer's Choice Award for "Top 10 Romantic Suspense of 2014" by *RT Book Reviews* and is a 2016 RWA RITA finalist. In addition to romance, he also writes thrillers, fantasy, and science fiction.

In among his career as a corporate project manager he has: rebuilt and single-handed a fifty-foot sailboat, both flown and jumped out of airplanes, designed and built two houses, and bicycled solo around the world.

He is now making his living as a full-time writer on the Oregon Coast with his beloved wife. He is constantly amazed at what you can do with a degree in Geophysics. You may keep up with his writing and receive exlusive content by subscribing to his newsletter at: www.mlbuchman.com.

*If you enjoyed this story,*
*you might also enjoy:*

## Target of the Heart (excerpt)
## -a Night Stalkers novel-

***Major Pete Napier hovered*** his MH-47G Chinook helicopter ten kilometers outside of Lhasa, Tibet and a mere two inches off the tundra. A mixed action team of Delta Force and The Activity—the slipperiest intel group on the planet—flung themselves aboard.

The additional load sent an infinitesimal shift in the cyclic control in his right hand. The hydraulics to close the rear loading ramp hummed through the entire frame of the massive helicopter. By the time his crew chief could reach forward to slap an "all secure" signal against his shoulder, they were already ten feet up and fifty out. That was enough altitude. He kept the nose down as he clawed for speed in the thin air at eleven thousand feet.

"Totally worth it," one of the D-boys announced as soon as he was on the Chinook's internal intercom.

He'd have to remember to tell that to the two Black Hawks flying guard for him…when they were in a friendly country and could risk a radio transmission. This deep inside China—or rather Chinese-held territory as the CIA's mission-briefing spook had insisted on calling it—radios attracted attention and were only used to avoid imminent death and destruction.

"Great, now I just need to get us out of this alive."

"Do that, Pete. We'd appreciate it."

He wished to hell he had a stealth bird like the one that had gone into bin Laden's compound. But the one that had crashed during that raid had been blown up. Where there was one, there were always two, but the second had gone back into hiding as thoroughly as if it had never existed. He hadn't heard a word about it since.

The Tibetan terrain was amazing, even if all he could see of it was the monochromatic green of night vision. And blackness. The largest city in Tibet lay a mere ten kilometers away and they were flying over barren wilderness. He could crash out here and no one would know for decades unless some yak herder stumbled upon them. Or were yaks in Mongolia? He was a corn-fed, white boy from Colorado, what did he know about Tibet? Most of the countries he'd flown into on black ops missions he'd only seen at night anyway.

While moving very, very fast.

Like now.

The inside of his visor was painted with overlapping readouts. A pre-defined terrain map, the best that modern satellite imaging could build made the first layer. This wasn't some crappy, on-line, look-at-a-picture-of-your-house display. Someone had a pile of dung outside their goat pen? He could see it, tell you how high it was, and probably say if they were pygmy goats or full-size LaManchas by the size of their shit-pellets if he zoomed in.

On top of that were projected the forward-looking infrared camera images. The FLIR imaging gave him a real-time overlay, in case someone had put an addition onto their goat shed since the last satellite pass, or parked their tractor across his intended flight path.

His nervous system was paying autonomic attention to that combined landscape. He also compensated for the thin air at altitude as he instinctively chose when to start his climb over said goat shed or his swerve around it.

It was the third layer, the tactical display that had most of his attention. At least he and the two Black Hawks flying escort on him were finally on the move.

To insert this deep into Tibet, without passing over Bhutan or Nepal, they'd had to add wingtanks on the Black Hawks' hardpoints where he'd much rather have a couple banks of

Hellfire missiles. Still, they had 20mm chain guns and the crew chiefs had miniguns which was some comfort.

While the action team was busy infiltrating the capital city and gathering intelligence on the particularly brutal Chinese assistant administrator, he and his crews had been squatting out in the wilderness under a camouflage net designed to make his helo look like just another god-forsaken Himalayan lump of granite.

Command had determined that it was better for the helos to wait on site through the day than risk flying out and back in. He and his crew had stood shifts on guard duty, but none of them had slept. They'd been flying together too long to have any new jokes, so they'd played a lot of cribbage. He'd long ago ruled no gambling on a mission, after a fistfight had broken out about a bluff hand that cost a Marine three hundred and forty-seven dollars. Marines hated losing to Army no matter how many times it happened. They'd had to sit on him for a long time before he calmed down.

Tonight's mission was part of an on-going campaign to discredit the Chinese "presence" in Tibet on the international stage—as if occupying the country the last sixty years didn't count toward ruling, whether invited or not. As usual, there was a crucial vote coming up at the U.N.—that, as usual, the Chinese could be guaranteed to ignore. However, the ever-hopeful CIA was in a hurry to make sure that any damaging information that they could validate was disseminated as thoroughly as possible prior to the vote.

Not his concern.

His concern was, were they going to pass over some Chinese sentry post at their top speed of a hundred and ninety-six miles an hour? The sentries would then call down a couple Shenyang J-16 jet fighters that could hustle along at Mach 2 to fry his sorry ass. He knew there was a pair of them parked at Lhasa along with some older gear that would be just as effective against his three helos.

"Don't suppose you could get a move on, Pete?"

"Eat shit, Nicolai!" He was a good man to have as a copilot. Pete knew he was holding on too tight, and Nicolai knew that a joke was the right way to ease the moment.

He, Nicolai, and the four pilots in the two Black Hawks had a long way to go tonight and he'd never make it if he stayed so tight on the controls that he could barely maneuver. Pete eased off and felt his fingers tingle with the rush of returning blood. They dove down into gorges and followed them as long as they dared. They hugged cliff walls at every opportunity to decrease their radar profile. And they climbed.

That was the true danger—they would be up near the helos' limits when they crossed over the backbone of the Himalayas in their rush for India. The air was so rarefied that they burned fuel at a prodigious rate. Their reserve didn't allow for any extended battles while crossing the border...not for any battle at all really.

# # #

It was pitch dark outside her helicopter when Captain Danielle Delacroix stamped on the left rudder pedal while giving the big Chinook right-directed control on the cyclic. It tipped her most of the way onto her side, but let her continue in a straight line. A Chinook's rotors were sixty feet across—front to back they overlapped to make the spread a hundred feet long. By cross-controlling her bird to tip it, she managed to execute a straight line between two mock pylons only thirty feet apart. They were made of thin cloth so they wouldn't down the helo if you sliced one—she was the only trainee to not have cut one yet.

At her current angle of attack, she took up less than a half-rotor of width, just twenty-four feet. That left her nearly three feet to either side, sufficient as she was moving at under a hundred knots.

The training instructor sitting beside her in the copilot's seat didn't react as she swooped through the training course at Fort Campbell, Kentucky. Only child of a single mother, she was used to providing her own feedback loops, so she didn't expect anything else. Those who expected outside validation rarely survived the SOAR induction testing, never mind the two years of training that followed.

As a loner kid, Danielle had learned that self-motivated congratulations and fun were much easier to come by than external ones. She'd spent innumerable hours deep in her mind as a pre-teen superheroine. At twenty-nine she was well on her way to becoming a real life one, though Helo-girl had never been a character she'd thought of in her youth.

External validation or not, after two years of training with the U.S. Army's 160th Special Operations Aviation Regiment she was ready for some action. At least *she* was convinced that she was. But the trainers of Fort Campbell, Kentucky had not signed off on anyone in her trainee class yet.

Nor had they given any hint of when they might.

She ducked ten tons of racing Chinook under a bridge and bounced into a near vertical climb to clear the power line on the far side. Like a ride on the toboggan at Terrassee Dufferin during *Le Carnaval de Québec,* only with five thousand horsepower at her finger-tips. Using her Army signing bonus—the first money in her life that was truly hers—to attend *Le Carnaval* had been her one trip back to her birthplace since her mother took them to America when she was ten.

To even apply to SOAR required five years of prior military rotorcraft experience. She had applied after seven years because of a chance encounter—or rather what she'd thought was a chance encounter at the time.

Captain Justin Roberts had been a top Chinook pilot, the one who had convinced her to switch from her beloved Black Hawk and try out the massive twin-rotor craft. One flight and she'd been a goner, begging her commander until he gave in and let her cross over to the new platform. Justin had made the jump from the 10th Mountain Division to the 160th SOAR not long after that.

Then one night she'd been having pizza in Watertown, New York a couple miles off the 10th's base at Fort Drum.

"Danielle?" Justin had greeted her with the surprise of finding a good friend in an unexpected place. Danielle had liked Justin— even if he was a too-tall, too-handsome cowboy and completely knew it. But "good friend" was unusual for Danielle, with anyone, and Justin came close.

"Captain Roberts," as a dry greeting over the top edge of her Suzanne Brockmann novel didn't faze him in the slightest.

"Mind if I join ya?" A question he then

answered for himself by sliding into the opposite seat and taking a slice of her pizza. She been thinking of taking the leftovers back to base, but that was now an idle thought.

"Are you enjoying life in SOAR?" she did her best to appear a normal, social human, a skill she'd learned by rote. *Greeting someone you knew after a time apart? Ask a question about them.* "They treating you well?"

"Whoo-ee, you have no idea, Danielle," his voice was smooth as...well, always...so she wouldn't think about it also sounding like a pickup line. He was beautiful, but didn't interest her; the outgoing ones never did.

"Tell me." *Men love to talk about themselves, so let them.*

And he did. But she'd soon forgotten about her novel, and would have forgotten the pizza if he hadn't reminded her to eat.

His stories shifted from intriguing to fascinating. There was a world out there that she'd been only peripherally aware of. The Night Stalkers of the 160th SOAR weren't simply better helicopter pilots, they were the most highly-trained and best-equipped ones on the planet. Their missions were pure razor's edge and black-op dark.

He'd left her with a hundred questions and enough interest to fill out an application to the 160th. Being a decent guy, Justin even paid for the pizza after eating half.

The speed at which she was rushed into testing told her that her meeting with Justin hadn't been by chance and that she owed him more than half a pizza next time they met. She'd asked after him a couple of times since she'd made it past the qualification exams— and the examiners' brutal interviews that had left her questioning her sanity, never mind her ability.

"Justin Roberts is presently deployed, ma'am," was the only response she'd ever gotten.

Now that she was through training—almost, had to be soon, didn't it?—Danielle realized that was probably less of an evasion and more likely to do with the brutal op tempo the Night Stalkers maintained. The SOAR 1st Battalion had just won the coveted Lt. General Ellis D. Parker awards for Outstanding Combat Aviation Battalion *and* Aviation Battalion of the Year. They'd been on deployment every single day of the last year, actually of the last decade-plus since 9/11.

The very first Special Forces boots on the ground in Afghanistan were delivered that October by the Night Stalkers and nothing had slacked off since. Justin might be in the 5th battalion D company, but they were just as heavily assigned as the 1st.

Part of their training had included tours in Afghanistan. But unlike their prior deployments, these were brief, intense, and then they'd be back in the States pushing to integrate their new skills.

SOAR needed her training to end and so did she.

Danielle was ready for the job, in her own, inestimable opinion. But she wasn't going to get there until the trainers signed off that she'd reached fully mission-qualified proficiency.

The Fort Campbell training course was never set up the same from one flight to the next, but it always had a time limit. The time would be short and they didn't tell you what it was. So she drove the Chinook for all it was worth like Regina Jaquess waterskiing her way to U.S. Ski Team Female Athlete of the Year.

The Night Stalkers were a damned secretive lot, and after two years of training, she understood why. With seven years flying for the 10th, she'd thought she was good.

She'd been repeatedly lauded as one of the top pilots at Fort Drum.

The Night Stalkers had offered an education in what it really meant to fly. In the two years of training, she'd flown more hours than in the seven years prior, despite two deployments to Iraq. And spent more time in the classroom than her life-to-date accumulated flight hours.

But she was ready now. It was *très viscérale,* right down in her bones she could feel it. The Chinook was as much a part of her nervous system as breathing.

Too bad they didn't build men the way they built the big Chinooks—especially the MH-47G which were built specifically to SOAR's requirements. The aircraft were steady, trustworthy, and the most immensely powerful helicopters deployed in the U.S. Army—what more could a girl ask for? But finding a superhero man to go with her superhero helicopter was just a fantasy for a lonely teenage girl.

She dove down into a canyon and slid to a hover mere inches over the reservoir inside the thirty-second window laid out on the flight plan.

Danielle resisted a sigh. She was ready for something to happen and to happen soon.

# # #

Pete's Chinook and his two escort Black Hawks crossed into the mountainous province of Sikkim, India ten feet over the glaciers and still moving fast. It was an hour before dawn, they'd made it out of China while it was still dark.

"Twenty minutes of fuel remaining," Nicolai said it like a personal challenge when they hit the border.

"Thanks, I never would have noticed."

It had been a nail-biting tradeoff: the more fuel he burned, the more easily he climbed due to the lighter load. The more he climbed, the faster he burned what little fuel remained.

Safe in Indian airspace he climbed hard as Nicolai counted down the minutes remaining, burning fuel even faster than he had been while crossing the mountains of southern Tibet. They caught up with the U.S. Air Force HC-130P Combat King refueling tanker with only ten minutes of fuel left.

"Ram that bitch," Nicolai called out.

Pete extended the refueling probe which reached only a few feet beyond the forward edge of the rotor blade and drove at the basket trailing behind the tanker on its long hose.

He nailed it on the first try despite the fluky winds. Striking the valve in the basket with over four hundred pounds of pressure, a clamp snapped over the refueling probe and Jet A fuel shot into his tanks.

His helo had the least fuel due to having the most men aboard, so he was first in line. His Number Two picked up the second refueling basket trailing off the other wing of the Combat King. Thirty seconds and three hundred gallons later and he was breathing much more easily.

"Ah," Nicolai sighed. "It is better than the sex," his thick Russian accent only ever surfaced in this moment or in a bar while picking up women.

"Hey, Nicolai," Nicky the Greek called over

the intercom from his crew chief position seated behind Pete. "Do you make love in Russian?"

A question Pete had always been careful to avoid.

"For you, I make special exception." That got a laugh over the system.

Which explained why Pete always kept his mouth shut at this moment.

"The ladies, Nicolai? What about the ladies?" Alfie the portside gunner asked.

"Ah," he sighed happily as he signaled that the other choppers had finished their refueling and formed up to either side, "the ladies love the Russian. They don't need to know I grew up in Maryland and I learn my great-great-grandfather's native tongue at the University called Virginia."

He sounded so pleased that Pete wished he'd done the same rather than study Japanese and Mandarin.

Another two hours of—thank god—straight-and-level flight at altitude through the breaking dawn and they landed on the aircraft carrier awaiting them in the Bay of Bengal. India had agreed to turn a blind eye as long as the Americans never actually touched their soil.

Once standing on the deck—and the worst of the kinks had been worked out—he pulled his team together: six pilots and seven crew chiefs.

"Honor to serve!" He saluted them sharply.

"Hell yeah!" They shouted in response and saluted in turn. It was their version of spiking the football in the end zone.

A petty officer in a bright green vest appeared at his elbow, "Follow me please, sir." He pointed toward the Navy-gray command structure that towered above the carrier's deck. The Commodore of the entire carrier group was waiting for him just outside the entrance. Not a good idea to keep a One-Star waiting, so he waved at the team.

"See you in the mess for dinner," he shouted to the crew over the noise of an F-18 Hornet fighter jet trapping on the #2 wire. After two days of surviving on MREs while squatting on the Tibetan tundra, he was ready for a steak, a burger, a mountain of pasta, whatever. Or maybe all three.

The green escorted him across the hazards

of the busy flight deck. Pete had kept his helmet on to buffer the noise, but even at that he winced as another Hornet fired up and was flung aloft by the catapult.

"Orders, Major Napier," the Commodore handed him a folded sheet the moment he arrived. "Hate to lose you."

The Commodore saluted, which Pete automatically returned before looking down at the sheet of paper in his hands. The man was gone before the import of Pete's orders slammed in.

A different green-clad deckhand showed up with Pete's duffle bag and began guiding him toward a loading C-2 Greyhound twin-prop airplane. It was parked number two for the launch catapult, close behind the raised jet-blast deflector.

His crew, being led across in the opposite direction to return to the berthing decks below, looked at him aghast.

"Stateside," was all he managed to gasp out as they passed.

A stream of foul cursing followed him from behind. Their crew was tight. Why the hell was Command breaking it up?

And what in the name of fuck-all had he done to deserve this?

He glanced at the orders again as he stumbled up the Greyhound's rear ramp and crash landed into a seat.

Training rookies?

It was worse than a demotion.

This was punishment.

*This and other titles are available at fine retailers everywhere.*

# Other works by M.L. Buchman

*By Break of Day*

*Newsletter signup at:*
*www.mlbuchman.com*